WE BOTH REA

Parent's Introduction

We Both Read is the first series of books designed to invite parents and children to share the reading of a story by taking turns reading aloud. This "shared reading" innovation, which was developed with reading education specialists, invites parents to read the more complex text and storyline on the left-hand pages. Children are encouraged to read the right-hand pages, which feature less complex text and storyline, specifically written for the beginning reader. You will note that a "talking parent" icon ⊜ precedes the parent's text and a "talking child" icon ⊙ precedes the child's text.

Reading aloud is one of the most important activities parents can share with their child to assist them in their reading development. However, *We Both Read* goes beyond reading *to* a child and allows parents to share the reading *with* a child. *We Both Read* is so powerful and effective because it combines two key elements in learning: "modeling" (the parent reads) and "doing" (the child reads). The result is not only faster reading development for the child, but a much more enjoyable and enriching experience for both!

You may find it helpful to read the entire book aloud yourself the first time, then invite your child to participate in the second reading. We encourage you to share and interact with your child as you read the book together. If your child is having difficulty, you might want to mention a few things to help them. "Sounding out" is good, but it will not work with all words. They can pick up clues about the words they are reading from the story, the context of the sentence, or even the pictures. Some stories have rhyming patterns that might help. For beginning readers, you also might want to suggest touching the words with their finger as they read, so they can better connect the voice sound and the printed word.

Sharing the *We Both Read* books together will engage you and your child in an interactive adventure in reading! It is a fun and easy way to encourage and help your child to read—and a wonderful way to start them off on a lifetime of reading enjoyment!

We Both Read: Frank and the Giant

_____

Text Copyright ©2005 by Dev Ross
Illustrations Copyright ©2005 Larry Reinhart
All rights reserved

Published by Treasure Bay, Inc.
40 Sir Francis Drake Boulevard
San Anselmo, CA 94960 USA

PRINTED IN SINGAPORE

Library of Congress Control Number: 2004112173

Hardcover ISBN-10: 1-891327-59-3
Hardcover ISBN-13: 978-1-891327-59-9
Paperback ISBN-10: 1-891327-60-7
Paperback ISBN-13: 978-1-891327-60-5

We Both Read® Books
Patent No. 5,957,693

Visit us online at:
www.webothread.com

WE BOTH READ®

Frank
and the Giant

By Dev Ross

Illustrated by Larry Reinhart

TREASURE BAY

Frank loves to play ball. He loves to throw his ball then hop after it.

Can you guess? Frank is . . .

. . . a frog.

When Frank throws the ball, his friend Mikey likes to bat it with his tail.

Can you guess? Mikey is . . .

. . . a mouse.

When Frank throws the ball and Mikey hits it with his tail, their friend Debby likes to fly up and catch it.

Can you guess? Debby is . . .

. . . a duck.

One day Frank threw the ball too hard. Mikey could not hit it. Debby could not catch it!

Away sailed . . .

. . . the ball.

The ball flew over a chicken.
The ball bounced between two bunnies.
The ball rolled under . . .

. . . a bird!

The friends happily chased the ball. Then it bounced someplace they did not want to go.

It bounced right into the giant's . . .

. . . house !

"Bye-bye, ball," said Debby.
"So long, ball," said Mikey.

But Frank didn't want to say good-bye.
He wanted his ball back! So he jumped
right through the giant's . . .

. . . window.

Frank looked up. He looked down. He looked all around. He did not see his ball.

But he did see a giant . . .

. . . chair.

Frank hopped up onto the big chair. But Frank still did not see his ball.

So, he jumped up higher to the giant . . .

. . . table.

Frank still did not see his ball.
But he did see a giant spoon and a giant . . .

. . . bowl.

Mikey and Debby leaned through the window to help Frank look. Then they heard someone coming.

It was . . .

. . . the giant!

Suddenly Frank felt very afraid. He didn't want the giant to see him, so he ran and hid under the giant's very large . . .

. . . spoon!

The giant poured himself a bowl of cereal. He started to eat, but was surprised to find something hanging from his spoon. He was surprised to see that it was a . . .

. . . frog!

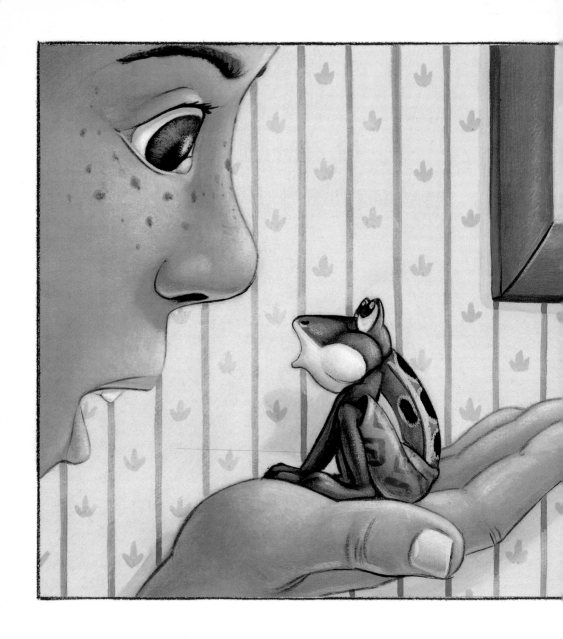

The giant looked at Frank the frog.
Frank the frog looked at the giant.
To Frank, the giant looked very, very . . .

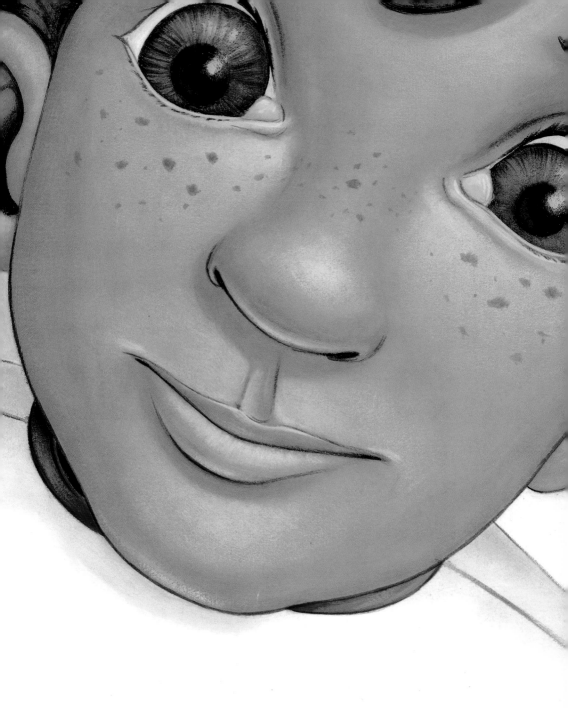

. . . BIG!

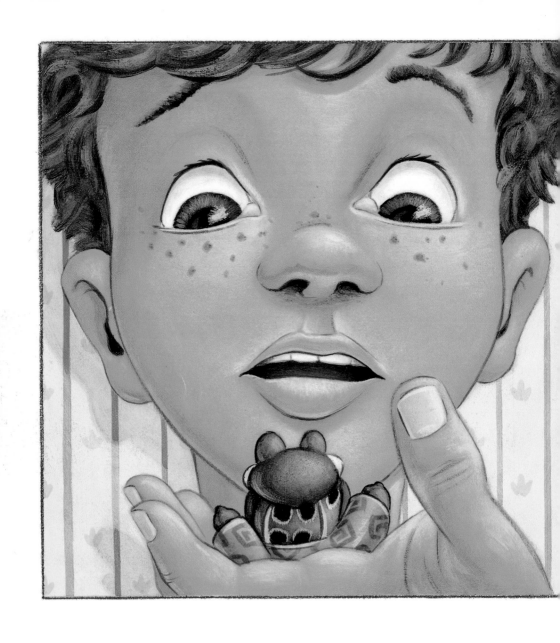

To the giant, Frank looked very, very . . .

. . . small.

The giant felt Frank's head. The giant
thought it was a very small head.

Frank felt the giant's head. Frank
thought it was a very . . .

. . . big head!

Frank felt his own nose.
It felt like a very little nose.

Frank felt the giant's nose.
It felt like a very large . . .

. . . nose.

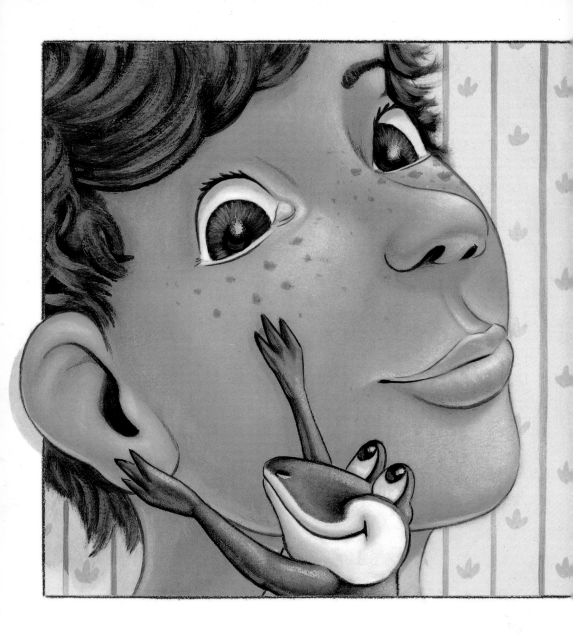

Frank saw that the giant also had two
very big ears, one very large mouth,
and lots and lots of very giant . . .

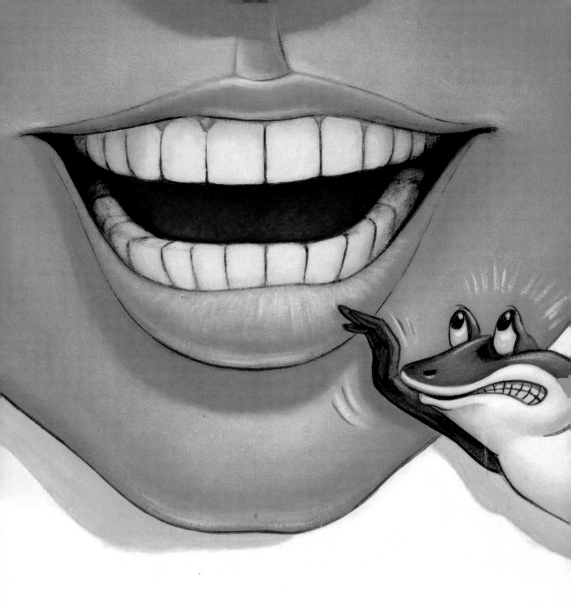

. . . teeth!

Frank pleaded, "Please don't eat me, big giant."

The giant replied with a grin, "I'm not a big giant. I'm just a little . . .

. . . boy!"

Frank and his friends were quite happy that the big giant was just a little boy. And they were even happier when the little boy helped them to find Frank's . . .

. . . ball.

If you liked *Frank and the Giant*, here are two other
We Both Read® Books you are sure to enjoy!

It is time for Lulu to be off to school, but she can't
find her shoes! All her little bug friends get off the
school bus to help her find them. Now everyone is
late, the frolicking searchers are messing up the house,
and Mother Ladybug is not very happy! Featuring a
lot of humor and a common situation that all children
can identify with, this book for the very beginning
reader is sure to be shared again and again!